GO BOTS

MIGHTY ROBOTS
MIGHTY VEHICLES

THE HIDEAWAY

Written by Rusty Hallock
Illustrated by Dan Spiegle

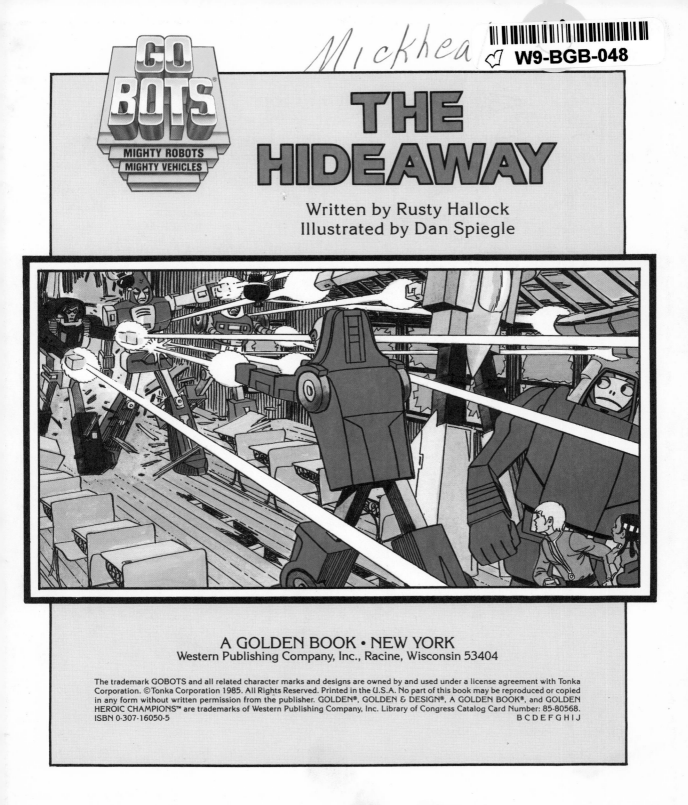

A GOLDEN BOOK • NEW YORK
Western Publishing Company, Inc., Racine, Wisconsin 53404

Scooter, the smallest of the Guardian GoBots, was returning to the *Command Center.* Suddenly he found himself surrounded by his enemies, Cy-Kill, Cop-Tur, and Crasher.

The three Renegade GoBots had left their home planet of GoBotron and come to Earth. They thought Earth would make a better base from which to conquer the world. Scooter, Leader-1, and Turbo had pursued them, in order to stop their evil designs.

"Now you're our prisoner," said Cy-Kill, the leader.

The Renegades' secret Earth ally, Professor Braxis, stood nearby. "Take him away before his friends come," he called out.

The Renegades locked Scooter in a secret cell with thick steel walls deep in the Operations Control warehouse of AstroCorps.

"You'll never get out of here unless your friends, Leader-1 and Turbo, agree to return to GoBotron—and leave Earth to us!" Cy-Kill said.

"If they refuse, we'll destroy everyone on Earth—beginning with you!" Crasher said with an evil laugh. "And thanks to Professor Braxis, we now have a way to do just that."

You're tough when you're talking to someone small.

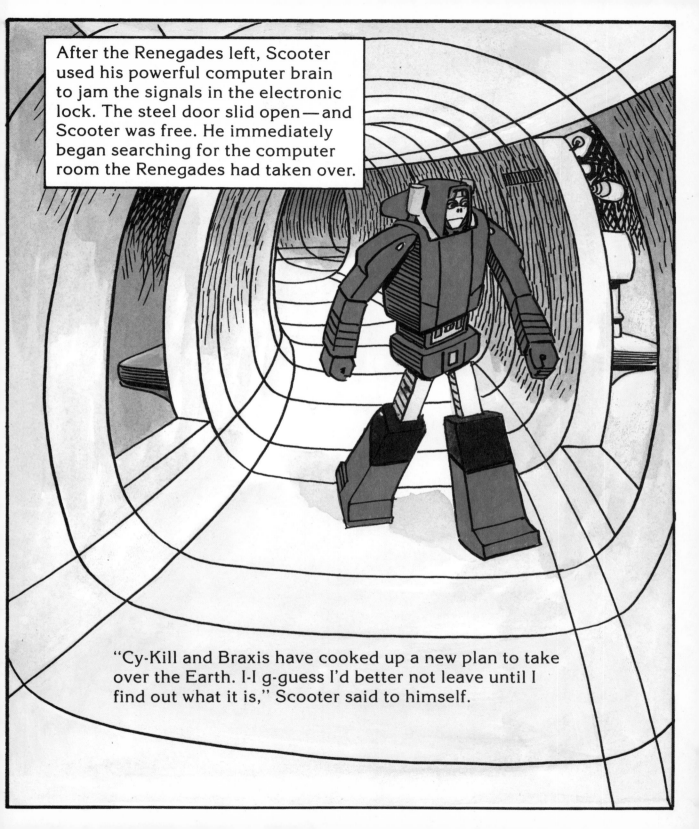

After the Renegades left, Scooter used his powerful computer brain to jam the signals in the electronic lock. The steel door slid open—and Scooter was free. He immediately began searching for the computer room the Renegades had taken over.

"Cy-Kill and Braxis have cooked up a new plan to take over the Earth. I-I g-guess I'd better not leave until I find out what it is," Scooter said to himself.

But as Scooter tapped into the computer, he heard footsteps coming his way. "Uh-oh, s-somebody's coming. I've got to h-hide!" Scooter said with a gulp.

Scooter was hiding behind some boxes when the door to the computer room opened. "Scooter, where are you?" a voice called. It was Leader-1! He and Turbo had come to rescue Scooter. Scooter didn't even ask how they found him.

The Guardians immediately returned to the *Command Center,* where their Earth friends — Captain Matt Hunter of AstroCorps and his young cadets, Nick Burns and A.J. Foster — were waiting.

"Stand by for the latest," Scooter said. "Cy-Kill and Professor Braxis have a new plan. All I found out is that it's called Operation Dark Net."

"Dark Net?!" Leader-1 said, looking alarmed. "I must send for the GoBot who invented the Dark Net Theory. Fortunately, the Astrobeam will bring him down from GoBotron quickly."

Suddenly, another GoBot beamed into the *Command Center*.

"Blaster!" Leader-1 said.

"Years ago, I invented a mathematical equation for creating a special force field," Blaster explained. "Using a system of lasers, I thought I could create an enormous, artificial black hole anywhere I wanted. It would suck into it everything that came near—meteors, satellites, spacecraft, even light beams. That's why I called it the Dark Net Theory. But before I could test my equation, Cy-Kill stole it from me."

DARK NET THEORY

"We need a hideaway," Leader-1 told Matt. "Someplace where Blaster can invent a device to knock out Operation Dark Net without being discovered."

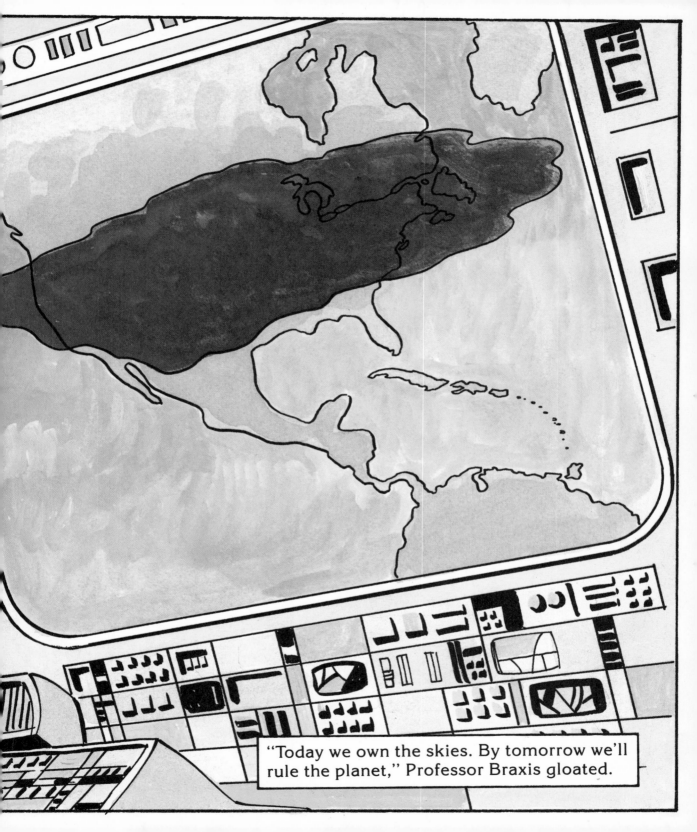

"Today we own the skies. By tomorrow we'll rule the planet," Professor Braxis gloated.

While the Renegades celebrated their evil victory, Matt was leaving the Operations Control warehouse, where he had gone to get parts for Blaster's invention. He had piled them aboard Leader-1 and sent him on ahead. Matt promised to return to the schoolhouse after checking out his space shuttle.

Suddenly he ran into Cy-Kill.

"This piece of scrap isn't on my shopping list," Matt said as he fired at the Renegade leader.

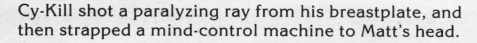

Cy-Kill shot a paralyzing ray from his breastplate, and then strapped a mind-control machine to Matt's head.

"Something tells me this isn't a hair dryer," Matt said. Suddenly Cy-Kill's voice filled Matt's mind.

"Captain Hunter, you will follow my orders exactly," Cy-Kill said. "I want you to go now and take your space shuttle for a test flight. You will be the guinea pig for the Dark Net! Ha ha ha!!"

Minutes later Matt climbed into the cockpit of the space shuttle. His eyes watched the dials and readouts. But his brain was on automatic pilot. Just as Cy-Kill had ordered, Matt was flying directly toward the Dark Net!

In their laboratory hideaway, Nick and A.J. noticed with alarm that Matt's spacecraft was on their monitor. He hadn't said anything about flying.

"Matt's flying straight for the Dark Net!" A.J. cried.

"Is the anti—Dark Net System ready?" Leader-1 called to Blaster.

"Almost. One more adjustment and I'll be able to turn the Dark Net off," Blaster said.

Blaster quickly finished his adjustments and turned the Dark Net off seconds before Matt was sucked into its depths.

When the Renegades saw that someone had defeated their fiendish plan, they were furious.

"Find out who did it!" Cy-Kill commanded Crasher.

"I've put out an electronic scan to find the source of the antilaser activity," said Crasher. "It seems to be coming from an abandoned schoolhouse."

"It must be those meddling Guardians!" Braxis said, pounding his fist.

"Then let's go teach them a lesson," Cop-Tur said cruelly as he changed into his helicopter form.

The Renegades burst into the schoolhouse hideaway.
"The Renegades!" Turbo shouted, leaping into action.
The room echoed with the noise of laser guns and energy bolts.
"I'm saving my strength," Scooter explained to A.J. and Nick.

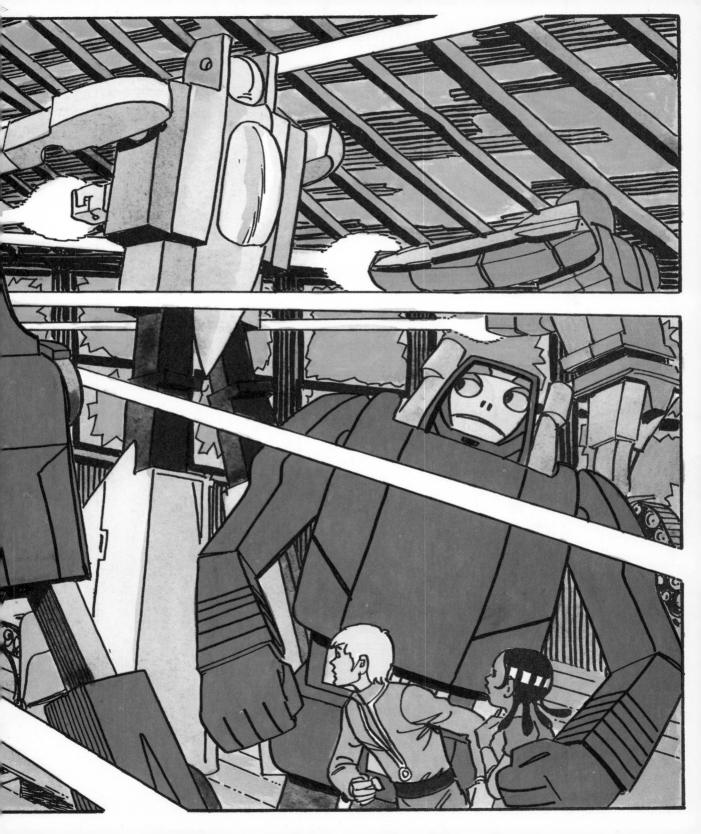

"We're outnumbered," Cy-Kill shouted when the battle was going against him.

"There's the anti—Dark Net system," Crasher said as she changed into her car form. "Watch me bash, smash, and trash it!"

She hit Blaster's invention at full speed—head-on!

He knew it was going to take every last bit of his energy to turn away from the black hole and bring Matt down to Earth.

"Well, let's not just sit around here waiting for the bad news," Turbo said, turning himself into a racing car. "Let's pay a visit to those Renegades!"

"Count me in," Blaster said. "If we can get my equation back, no one will ever have to worry about Operation Dark Net again."

Once again the Guardians raided the Operations Control warehouse and a nervous Scooter quickly picked the Renegade computer's brain.

Then Blaster and Turbo slammed into the Operation Dark Net system, destroying it for good.

Back in the *Command Center,* Leader-1 and Matt were safe and sound.

"You risked your life for me," Matt said, thanking Leader-1. "I hope I can repay you someday."

"No, it is I who wish to repay *you* for the friendship you've given us here on Earth," Leader-1 said.

Then they all turned to say good-by to Blaster, who faded back to GoBotron as his time on Earth came to an end.